CANADA

Ellesmere Island

Baffin Island

Iqaluit ★

ATLANTIC OCEAN

ROUTE

—— by plane
•••• by water
- - - by train
〰 by car/
motorcycle

Hudson Bay

MANITOBA

NEWFOUNDLAND AND
LABRADOR

QUÉBEC

ONTARIO

St. Lawrence River

PRINCE
EDWARD
ISLAND

St. John's

Lake Huron

Québec City ★

Charlottetown ★

Fredericton ★

Lake Superior

Ottawa ★

Montréal ●

Saint John ●

Halifax ★

Lake Michigan

Toronto ★

Lake Ontario

NEW BRUNSWICK

NOVA SCOTIA

Lake Erie

Niagara Falls

Bay of Fundy

The Twelve Days of Christmas in Canada

written by **Ellen Warwick**

illustrated by **Kim Smith**

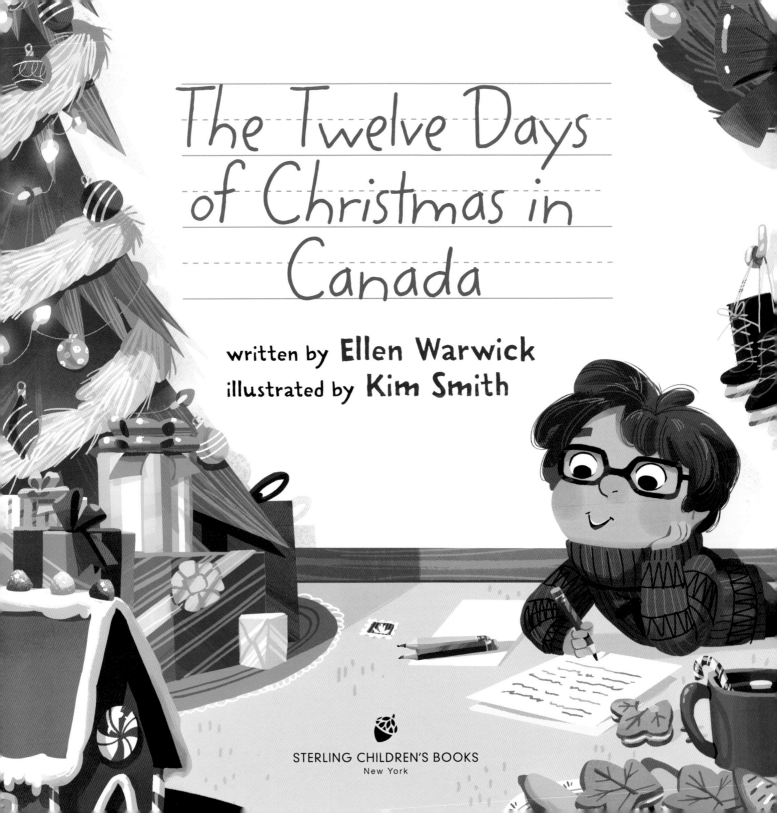

STERLING CHILDREN'S BOOKS
New York

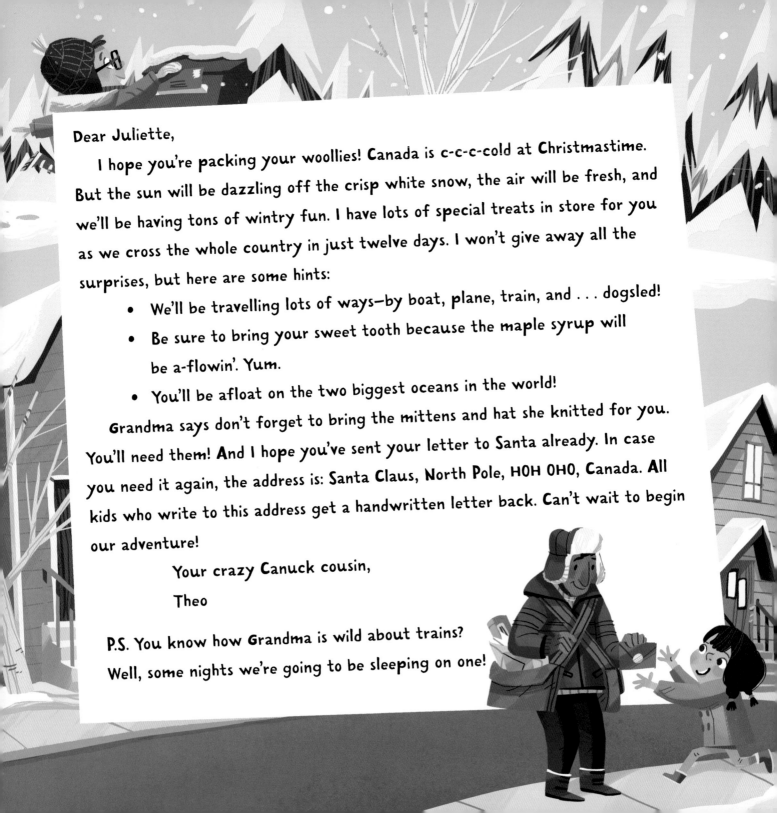

Dear Juliette,

I hope you're packing your woollies! Canada is c-c-c-cold at Christmastime. But the sun will be dazzling off the crisp white snow, the air will be fresh, and we'll be having tons of wintry fun. I have lots of special treats in store for you as we cross the whole country in just twelve days. I won't give away all the surprises, but here are some hints:

- We'll be travelling lots of ways—by boat, plane, train, and . . . dogsled!
- Be sure to bring your sweet tooth because the maple syrup will be a-flowin'. Yum.
- You'll be afloat on the two biggest oceans in the world!

Grandma says don't forget to bring the mittens and hat she knitted for you. You'll need them! And I hope you've sent your letter to Santa already. In case you need it again, the address is: Santa Claus, North Pole, H0H 0H0, Canada. All kids who write to this address get a handwritten letter back. Can't wait to begin our adventure!

Your crazy Canuck cousin,

Theo

P.S. You know how Grandma is wild about trains? Well, some nights we're going to be sleeping on one!

Dear Mom,

I arrived safe and sound in Charlottetown! As soon as they saw me, Grandma and Theo gave me the biggest bear hug I've ever had. It sure was great to see them at last. On the way in from the airport, Theo told me that Charlottetown is on an island—Prince Edward Island—and you're never more than 30 minutes away from the beach anywhere you go here. With rolling hills, white sand beaches, red cliffs, and ocean coves, it's no wonder L.M. Montgomery was inspired to write her world-famous <u>Anne of Green Gables</u> books here. I felt like I'd stepped into one of them and that Anne and I would soon be "kindred spirits."

We headed straight downtown into the twinkling lights of Historic Charlottetown, which looked as pretty as an old-fashioned Christmas card. Then, on to Peake's Wharf Historic Waterfront and a jaunt over to Blockhouse Point Lighthouse, where I finally got to see the Atlantic Ocean. Wow! It's so enormous! But I also saw the <u>strangest</u> thing: a loon in a maple tree. And maybe my eyes were tricking me, but I am sure the loon winked at Theo. What is he up to?

Curious in Charlottetown,
Juliette

On the first day of Christmas,
my cousin gave to me . . .

a loon in a
maple tree.

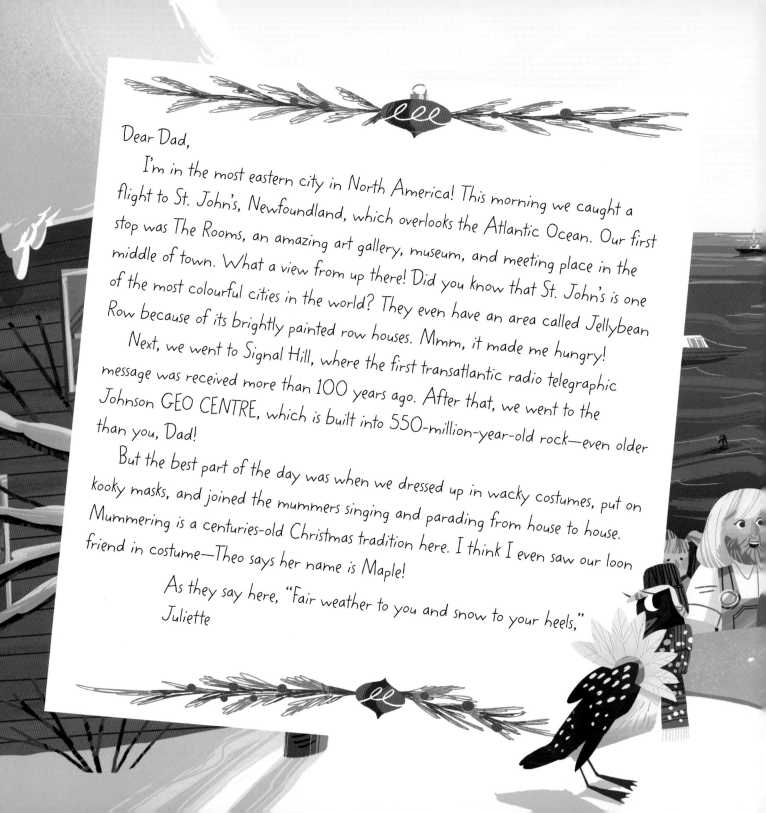

Dear Dad,

I'm in the most eastern city in North America! This morning we caught a flight to St. John's, Newfoundland, which overlooks the Atlantic Ocean. Our first stop was The Rooms, an amazing art gallery, museum, and meeting place in the middle of town. What a view from up there! Did you know that St. John's is one of the most colourful cities in the world? They even have an area called Jellybean Row because of its brightly painted row houses. Mmm, it made me hungry!

Next, we went to Signal Hill, where the first transatlantic radio telegraphic message was received more than 100 years ago. After that, we went to the Johnson GEO CENTRE, which is built into 550-million-year-old rock—even older than you, Dad!

But the best part of the day was when we dressed up in wacky costumes, put on kooky masks, and joined the mummers singing and parading from house to house. Mummering is a centuries-old Christmas tradition here. I think I even saw our loon friend in costume—Theo says her name is Maple!

As they say here, "Fair weather to you and snow to your heels,"
Juliette

On the second day of Christmas,
my cousin gave to me . . .

2 mummers' masks

and a loon in a maple tree.

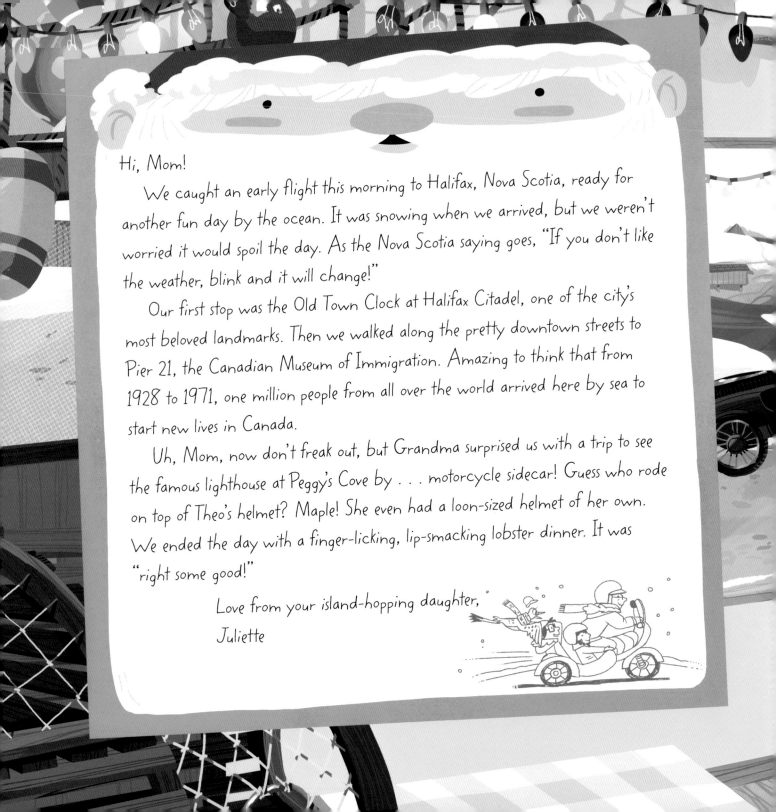

Hi, Mom!

We caught an early flight this morning to Halifax, Nova Scotia, ready for another fun day by the ocean. It was snowing when we arrived, but we weren't worried it would spoil the day. As the Nova Scotia saying goes, "If you don't like the weather, blink and it will change!"

Our first stop was the Old Town Clock at Halifax Citadel, one of the city's most beloved landmarks. Then we walked along the pretty downtown streets to Pier 21, the Canadian Museum of Immigration. Amazing to think that from 1928 to 1971, one million people from all over the world arrived here by sea to start new lives in Canada.

Uh, Mom, now don't freak out, but Grandma surprised us with a trip to see the famous lighthouse at Peggy's Cove by . . . motorcycle sidecar! Guess who rode on top of Theo's helmet? Maple! She even had a loon-sized helmet of her own. We ended the day with a finger-licking, lip-smacking lobster dinner. It was "right some good!"

Love from your island-hopping daughter,
Juliette

Hello, Dad.

I became a seafaring girl when we took a Bay of Fundy ferry to Saint John, New Brunswick, this morning. Just as Theo promised, we were afloat on the Atlantic Ocean, and it was awesome! The Bay of Fundy has the highest tides in the world, with 100 billion tons of water flowing in and out twice every day. I think I may have seen a whale's tail in the distance—maybe it was the giant whale from the Mi'kmaq First Nations legend! Remind me to tell you the whole incredible story when I get home.

After we docked, we made our way to New Brunswick's capital, Fredericton. Even though the City Hall Clock Tower is normally closed in the winter, Grandma called ahead and made a special appointment for us. We had the Clock Tower all to ourselves! We climbed to the top for a great view, and then spun on the human gyroscope at Science East. I think I'm still dizzy from that! Then, we step-danced till we dropped to the fiddle music at a <u>ceilidh</u> (sounds like kay-lee)—an Acadian party. They sure have lots of <u>joie de vivre</u>!

On the way to catch the train in Moncton, we went to Magnetic Hill. Grandma drove to the bottom of the hill and a natural force seemed to pull our car all the way back up to the top again! Now that's power. Even Maple was amazed!

Love from your magnetic daughter,
Juliette

On the fourth day of Christmas,
my cousin gave to me . . .

4 fiddles wild

3 lobsters, 2 mummers' masks,
and a loon in a maple tree.

Chère Maman,

When we found our seats on the train last night, I was a little curious. How could we sleep sitting up? Gosh, was I surprised when Grandma folded beds down from the wall for us! The gentle rocking of the train had us all asleep in no time. When we woke, we were in Montréal, Québec!

French is spoken all over Canada, but in Québec, it's the official language. And I sure can see why Québec is called <u>la belle province</u>. With its twinkling lights, beautiful architecture, and enticing bakeries, I felt like I had stepped into a magical snow globe. From the cozy seat of a horse-drawn carriage, we toured along the St. Lawrence River to Old Montréal and then to a traditional outdoor Christmas market. The maple sugar cotton candy was so good!

No trip to Montréal is complete without poutine—French fries smothered in gravy and cheese curds. And we also stopped at a bagel bakery to order five of Montréal's world-famous, wood-fired bagels. (One for Maple, too!) <u>Délicieux!</u>

    À bientôt,
    Juliette

P.S. Did you know that Québec produces 77% of the world's supply of maple syrup, and millions of kilograms are stored here at the International Strategic Reserve? Syrup is a serious—and seriously good—business here!

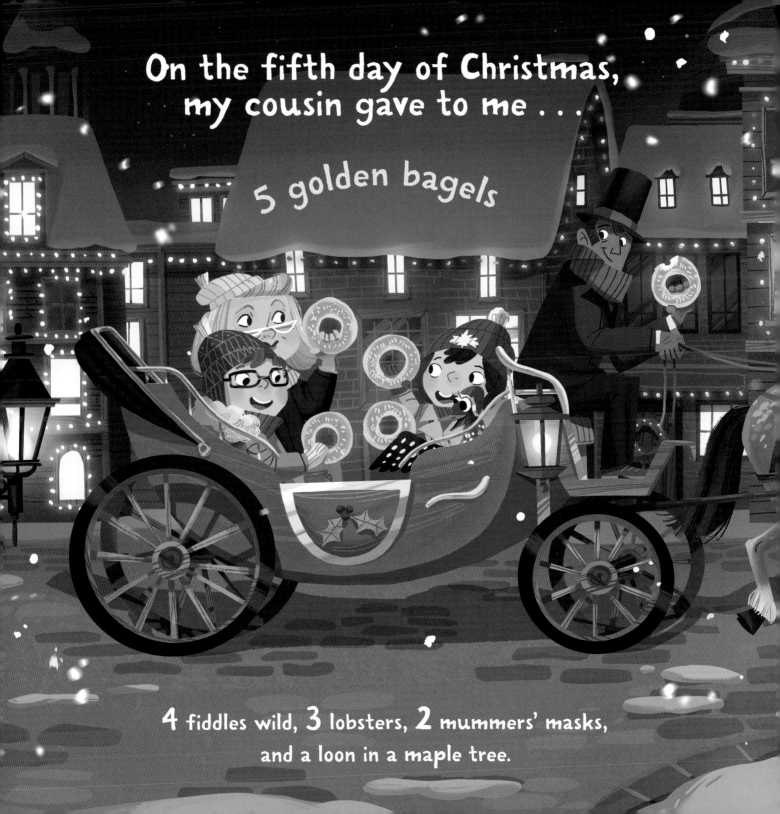

On the fifth day of Christmas,
my cousin gave to me . . .

5 golden bagels

4 fiddles wild, 3 lobsters, 2 mummers' masks,
and a loon in a maple tree.

Greetings, Dad!

Would you believe I ate a beaver tail today?! This morning, after a quick train trip, we arrived at Canada's capital, Ottawa, Ontario. Then we strapped on our skates to glide along the world's biggest skating rink, the Rideau Canal. Grandma and Maple weren't too steady on their skates, so Theo and I pushed them in a rented red sleigh. We were rewarded with a stop at a food shack right on the ice for hot chocolate and beaver tails, which are like flattened donuts. Yummy, eh? (I'm starting to sound like a Canadian! <u>Everyone</u> says "eh" here, which sounds like the letter "A.")

Then we took Maple to the Royal Canadian Mint to see how one-dollar coins are made. Maple loves that they're called "loonies" because of the loon image on one side. I wonder if she was the model for them. Later, we checked out the Group of Seven and First Nations artwork at the National Gallery of Canada. Inspiring!

The sun sets early here in winter, so we checked out the thousands of shimmering lights on Parliament Hill and were thrilled to see marching Mounties in their brilliant Red Serge jackets. The Royal Canadian Mounted Police, or Mounties, have been protecting the people of Canada since 1873!

Awesome, eh?

Juliette

On the sixth day of Christmas,
my cousin gave to me . . .

6 Mounties marching

5 golden bagels, 4 fiddles wild,
3 lobsters, 2 mummers' masks,
and a loon in a maple tree.

Hello, Bonjour, Ciao, Shalom, Ni Hao, Namaste, Hola, Privet, Oi, Mom!

Here I am, after another terrific train ride, in Canada's largest and the world's most multicultural city: Toronto, Ontario. There's a neighbourhood here for everybody, including two Little Italy areas, Koreatown, Little India, and SIX Chinatowns! And, because almost half of the people here were born outside the country, you can find the most amazing food and restaurants from around the globe.

After eating Toronto's favourite meal, brunch (with plenty of maple syrup!), we went to Casa Loma, a real castle right in the middle of the city. Feeling like a queen in the tower, I could see all the way down to Lake Ontario. Then we listened to one of the coolest sounds of the city—streetcars ringing their bells—as we rode to North America's highest structure, the CN Tower. Wow, looking down through the glass floor on the observation deck, we were 342 metres (1,122 feet) above the ground!

As the sun set, we drove along the shore of Lake Ontario to the Niagara Falls Winter Festival of Lights. The largest waterfall in North America was lit up with rainbow lights and spectacular fireworks. Breathtaking!

Love from your awestruck daughter,
Juliette

P.S. Maple considered going over the falls in a barrel, but she changed her mind. Thank goodness! I love this loony loon.

On the seventh day of Christmas,
my cousin gave to me . . .

7 streetcars ringing

6 Mounties marching, 5 golden bagels,
4 fiddles wild, 3 lobsters, 2 mummers' masks,
and a loon in a maple tree.

Hi, Dad.

We travelled our longest distance by plane last night to get to Winnipeg, Manitoba. The view from the plane was not just amazing—it was out of this world! We were dazzled by the aurora borealis (that's the fancy name for the northern lights). Arcs and streams of red and green light shot up from the horizon. So festive!

When we landed, our first stop was The Forks, a historic meeting place at the fork of the two rivers in Winnipeg: the Assiniboine and the Red Rivers. We had a blast at the markets, museums, parks, and The Forks Market Tower, where we could see Winnipeg's skyline and the spot where the rivers converge. Beginning with the First Nations, people have been meeting here for more than 6,000 years!

I bet you've never had a polar bear swim over your head. I have! Grandma, Theo, and I stood inside a see-through tunnel at the bottom of the pool at the Assiniboine Park Zoo's arctic exhibit while polar bears swam all around us, zipping and frolicking. In those icy waters, they sure are cool!

Your bear-y happy daughter,

Juliette

P.S. Tonight at the Royal Winnipeg Ballet's "Nutcracker," Maple leapt onto the stage and joined the show. She looked awesome en pointe!

On the eighth day of Christmas,
my cousin gave to me . . .

8 bears a-swimming

7 streetcars ringing, 6 Mounties marching,
5 golden bagels, 4 fiddles wild,
3 lobsters, 2 mummers' masks,
and a loon in a maple tree.

Dear Mom,

After another cozy trip on the train, speeding past the vast prairie lands and the enormous starry sky, we arrived in Saskatoon, Saskatchewan. The city was named after the delicious berries that grow around here. Saskatoon berry jam is so yummy—kind of like very tasty blueberries. I popped a jar in my suitcase for you, my jam-lovin' mom.

Today, I learned how to mush. Nope, not how to squish stuff! What I mean is that I learned how to be a dogsled driver, also called a "musher." The husky dogs were so excited to start running they howled and leapt in the air, and when it was finally time to go, they took off like a shot for our exhilarating ride through the boreal forest. Mushers have a lingo all their own that the dogs understand: "Hike!" "Gee!" "Haw!" (That means, "Let's go!" "Turn right!" "Turn left!")

When it started to get dark, we rode on a horse-drawn wagon through the sparkling Enchanted Forest Holiday Light Tour at the Saskatoon Forest Farm Park and Zoo. Magical!

And guess where we slept last night? In a traditional First Nations tipi on the plains at Wanuskewin Heritage Park! Before turning in, we ate bannock (fry bread) and drank hot chocolate while listening to stories by the warm campfire.

Love,
Musher Juliette

P.S. After watching a First Nations Hoop Dance, Maple jumped right in, but it didn't go quite as well as she'd hoped!

On the ninth day of Christmas, my cousin gave to me . . .

9 sled dogs howling

8 bears a-swimming, 7 streetcars ringing, 6 Mounties marching, 5 golden bagels, 4 fiddles wild, 3 lobsters, 2 mummers' masks, and a loon in a maple tree.

Dear Dad,

Yee-haw! Caught a flight this morning to Calgary, Alberta, which is Canada's Wild West. First stop: cowboy hats and boots for each of us. Maple was kicking up her heels! Who knew she could ride a mechanical bull?!

Hey Dad, you know those terrifyingly fast luge sleds you love watching during the Winter Olympics? Well, I learned to drive one at WinSport's Canada Olympic Park. Fastest speed: 60 kilometres (37 miles) per hour. Oh, yeah! Olympics, here I come!

This afternoon we headed out of town to check out the hoodoos (mushroom-shaped rock formations) and the Drumheller Valley Dinosaur Trail in the Canadian Badlands. This is one of the biggest dinosaur fossil sites in the world. There are even dinosaurs named <u>Albertosaurus</u> and <u>Edmontosaurus</u> because they were discovered right here. We were awestruck when we saw them displayed at the amazing Royal Tyrrell Museum of Palaeontology, which is packed with humungous dinosaur fossils. It made me want to ROAR!!!

We capped off this awesome day back in Calgary at a heart-thumping, foot-stomping, crowd-cheering hockey game—Canada's favourite sport! The players were on fire!

She shoots, she scores!
Juliette

On the tenth day of Christmas,
my cousin gave to me . . .

10 players skating

9 sled dogs howling, 8 bears a-swimming, 7 streetcars ringing,
6 Mounties marching, 5 golden bagels, 4 fiddles wild,
3 lobsters, 2 mummers' masks, and a loon in a maple tree.

Hey, Mom.

Just like the saying goes, "Beautiful British Columbia" sure is! After an early morning flight, we were thrilled to arrive in Vancouver, British Columbia, nestled between the Rocky Mountains and the Pacific Ocean. We went straight to Granville Island to get some delicious breakfast treats at the many market stalls. Next we checked out historic Gastown, with its cobblestone streets, and the Gastown Steam Clock, which runs on steam from the city's underground heating system. What a gas!

We passed gigantic totem poles in Stanley Park, went across Lions Gate Bridge, and rode up Grouse Mountain on the Skyride, North America's biggest aerial tram. The view was stunning: we could see the city of Vancouver, the Pacific Ocean, the Gulf Islands, and a bunch of snowy Rocky Mountain peaks! We geared up and hit the snowboarding terrain park to shred the jibs and jumps. Maple's ollies off the quarter-pipe were magical!

As the sun fell, we defied gravity crossing the Capilano Suspension Bridge—70 metres (230 feet) above the rainforest floor. Surrounded by hundreds of thousands of Christmas lights, and the world's largest living Christmas tree, the canyon below us was brilliant!

Your daring daughter,
Juliette

On the eleventh day of Christmas,
my cousin gave to me . . .

11 snowboards shredding

10 players skating, 9 sled dogs howling, 8 bears a-swimming,
7 streetcars ringing, 6 Mounties marching, 5 golden bagels,
4 fiddles wild, 3 lobsters, 2 mummers' masks,
and a loon in a maple tree.

Hi, Dad!

I'm a seafarer again! This morning we took a Pacific Ocean ferry to Victoria, British Columbia, which is on Vancouver Island and is our last and most western stop. We made it ALL the way across Canada!

Victoria has the mildest weather in the country, which is why it's called the City of Gardens. It made sense that we started off the day admiring the Christmas displays at The Butchart Gardens, which has lots of greenery even in winter! From there, we hopped on a whale-watching tour boat. Once we were out at sea, the most incredible thing happened: twelve orca whales leapt out of the water at once! Our guide said she had NEVER seen anything like it.

Later we headed to Victoria's Inner Harbour, where boats and seaplanes dock. Overlooking the Harbour is the Fairmont Empress Hotel, which is world famous for its afternoon tea. It was delicious, but when we weren't looking, SOMEONE gobbled up all the Nanaimo bars. Maple! Tsk, tsk!

Nighttime at the Harbour was dazzling. Carollers sang and all the buildings and boats were draped in glittering lights that sparkled off the water. It was a stunning end to an amazing trip!

Don't forget to bring the truck when you pick me up at the airport tomorrow—I'm... uh... bringing home a lot of souvenirs.

Your Canuck-crazy kid,

Juliette

P.S. Our next family trip has just GOT to be to Canada's northern territories: Yukon, Northwest Territories, and Nunavut. The far north is calling me!

On the twelfth day of Christmas, my cousin gave to me . . .

12 orcas breaching

11 snowboards shredding, 10 players skating, 9 sled dogs howling, 8 bears a-swimming, 7 streetcars ringing, 6 Mounties marching, 5 golden bagels, 4 fiddles wild, 3 lobsters, 2 mummers' masks, and a loon in a maple tree.

Canada: From Sea to Sea

Capital: Ottawa, Ontario • **National Abbreviation:** CA • **Largest City:** Toronto, Ontario • **National Animal:** the beaver • **National Tree:** the maple tree • **National Motto:** *A Mari Usque Ad Mare* (From Sea to Sea) • **National Anthem:** *O Canada* • **National Colours:** red and white • **National Sports:** ice hockey in winter, lacrosse in summer • **National Horse:** the Canadian horse • **Official Languages:** English and French • **Size:** 9,984,670 sq km (3,855,103 sq mi)

Some Amazing Canadians:

First Nations, Inuit, and Métis Peoples: Descending from the first people of Canada going back at least 12,000 years, there are currently over 630 recognized groups of indigenous people, with varying cultural traditions, in different regions of Canada. There are many indigenous languages spoken in Canada, including Lillooet, Innu, Ojibwe, Haida, Mi'kmaq, Algonquin, and Gwich'in.

Canadian Comedians: Canadians are hilarious! Here are some of the famous ones: Mike Myers, Jim Carrey, Martin Short, Dan Aykroyd, John Candy, and Catherine O'Hara.

Dr. Roberta Bondar (1945–), Canada's first woman in space, is a neurologist who headed an international space medicine team at NASA. She is also a published author and artist. She's won many awards, including the Order of Canada and the NASA Space Flight Medal. She has been inducted into the Canadian Medical Hall of Fame and holds twenty-four honourary doctorates.

Terry Fox (1958–1981) lost his leg to cancer at the age of eighteen. He wanted to help end the suffering of other Canadians with cancer so he started the Marathon of Hope, a race across Canada to raise money for research. Terry made it from St. John's, Newfoundland, to Thunder Bay, Ontario, before succumbing to lung cancer and passing away at age twenty-two. Every year since, Canadians have participated in the Terry Fox Run and have raised over $650 million to date.

Craig Kielburger (1982–) was outraged when he read a tragic newspaper story about a young Pakistani boy, Iqbal Masih, who was enslaved in a carpet factory from the age of four. Craig felt compelled to do something. At age twelve, he founded *Free the Children* to empower young people to help other young people. The international charity has worked in 45 countries and involves 2.3 million children who want to make the world a better place.

Awesome Canadian Inventions:

- James Naismith, a native of Almonte, Ontario, invented basketball in 1891. The first basket he used was a peach basket!
- Alexander Graham Bell invented the telephone in 1876 in Brantford, Ontario.
- Frederick Banting and Charles Best discovered and extracted insulin in 1921 in Toronto, Ontario, and then used it to successfully treat people with diabetes. Banting won the Nobel Prize in Medicine in 1923.
- Other weird and wonderful Canadian inventions include five-pin bowling, the paint roller, the snowblower, instant mashed potatoes, the green garbage bag, and the goalie mask.

Cool Canadian Records:

- Once the world's largest shopping mall, the West Edmonton Mall in Alberta still has the world's largest parking lot. With 20,000 spots, you'd better not forget where you parked!
- The world's tallest recorded female was Anna Haining Bates, who measured 2.29 metres (7 feet, 6 inches). Anna was born in Nova Scotia in 1846. Too bad they didn't have basketball back then. She would have been a star player!
- The world's largest coin is the Big Nickel in Sudbury, Ontario. It's 9 metres (30 feet) tall.
- Yonge Street in Toronto is 1896 kilometres (1,178 miles) long, and the longest street in the world (although some say this is up for debate). Canada also has the world's longest national highway. The Trans-Canada Highway runs from Victoria, British Columbia, to St John's, Newfoundland, and is 7821 kilometres (4,860 miles) long.

Wacky Canadian Landmarks:

- Hailing all Trekkies! Beam down to Vulcan, Alberta, to see a five-tonne replica of the *USS Starship Enterprise*, which measures 9.4 metres (31 feet) long and 2.7 metres (9 feet) high.
- The world's largest hockey stick, 62 metres (203 feet) long, is in Duncan, British Columbia. And just in case someone very large wants to use it, there's a huge puck to go with it.
- The Easter Bunny must have had a humongous basket when it delivered the world's biggest Easter egg, or pysanka, in Vegreville, Alberta. At 9 metres (30 feet) long and weighing 2.5 tonnes, it's egg-ceptional!

- The world's largest Muskoka chair is in Gravenhurst, Ontario, measuring 6.4 metres (21 feet) high. Don't worry if you miss it, though. There are lots more giant Muskoka chairs in Ontario, in Varney, Thessalon, South River, Moose Lake, Huntsville, Cloyne, Fort Erie, and Bethany. And if you want to try a different kind of chair, check out the giant rocking chair in Fowlers Corners, Ontario, the giant chair and side table in La Bostonnais, Québec, or the large purple chair in Truro, Nova Scotia.

- Try not to get pinched when you sit on the biggest lobster sculpture in the world in Shediac, New Brunswick. Measuring 11 metres (36 feet) long and 5 metres (16 feet) high, it's a good thing this 90-tonne monster (including the pedestal) is only a statue!

Astounding Canadian History:

- The first permanent Canadian settlement was founded in 1604, but the Vikings, or Norse, were the first group to arrive from Europe around 1000 CE. You can still visit their dwellings at L'Anse aux Meadows, Newfoundland. And the very first people to arrive in what is now Canada were Siberians who came across the Bering land bridge during an ice age around 13,000 BCE. Whoa, long time ago!

- July 5, 1937, was the hottest recorded day in Canada ever! The temperature reached a scorching 45°C (113°F) in the towns of Midale and Yellow Grass, Saskatchewan. But it's not always so hot here. The coldest temperature ever recorded in Canada was -63°C (-81.4°F) in Snag, Yukon, on February 3, 1947.

- Play ball! The oldest Canadian baseball field (and perhaps the oldest field in the world) was built in 1877 in London, Ontario, and named Tecumseh Park. Now called Labatt Park, this baseball diamond is still in use today.

Glorious Canadian Nature:

- The eastern white cedar tree is one of the slowest-growing trees in the world. Usually living to about 200 years, some as old as 1300 years have been found in Ontario.

- Water, water, everywhere! Canada has an estimated 60% of all of the world's lakes—about three million of them!

- The beautiful, white- or cream-coloured Kermode bear, also known as the spirit bear or ghost bear, is unique to Canada. A subspecies of the North American black bear, they live in British Columbia's coastal rainforests.

- If you love snakes, head to the Narcisse Snake Dens north of Winnipeg, Manitoba. Every spring, tens of thousands of red-sided garter snakes slither out of their dens to mate.

To Emma, my favourite person in the world. —xox, Ellen

For my mom and dad, and Eric. —K. S.

STERLING CHILDREN'S BOOKS
New York

An Imprint of Sterling Publishing
1166 Avenue of the Americas
New York, NY 10036

STERLING CHILDREN'S BOOKS and the distinctive Sterling Children's Books logo are trademarks of Sterling Publishing Co., Inc.

Text © 2015 by Ellen Warwick
Illustrations © 2015 by Kim Smith
The illustrations in this book were created digitally.
Designed by Andrea Miller.

ISBN 978-1-4549-1431-0

Distributed in Canada by Sterling Publishing
c/o Canadian Manda Group, 664 Annette Street
Toronto, Ontario, Canada M6S 2C8
Distributed in the United Kingdom by GMC Distribution Services
Castle Place, 166 High Street, Lewes, East Sussex, England BN7 1XU
Distributed in Australia by Capricorn Link (Australia) Pty. Ltd.
P.O. Box 704, Windsor, NSW 2756, Australia

For information about custom editions, special sales, and premium and corporate purchases,
please contact Sterling Special Sales at 800-805-5489 or specialsales@sterlingpublishing.com.

Manufactured in China
Lot #:
2 4 6 8 10 9 7 5 3
06/16

www.sterlingpublishing.com/kids